Ce Livre
Appartient à

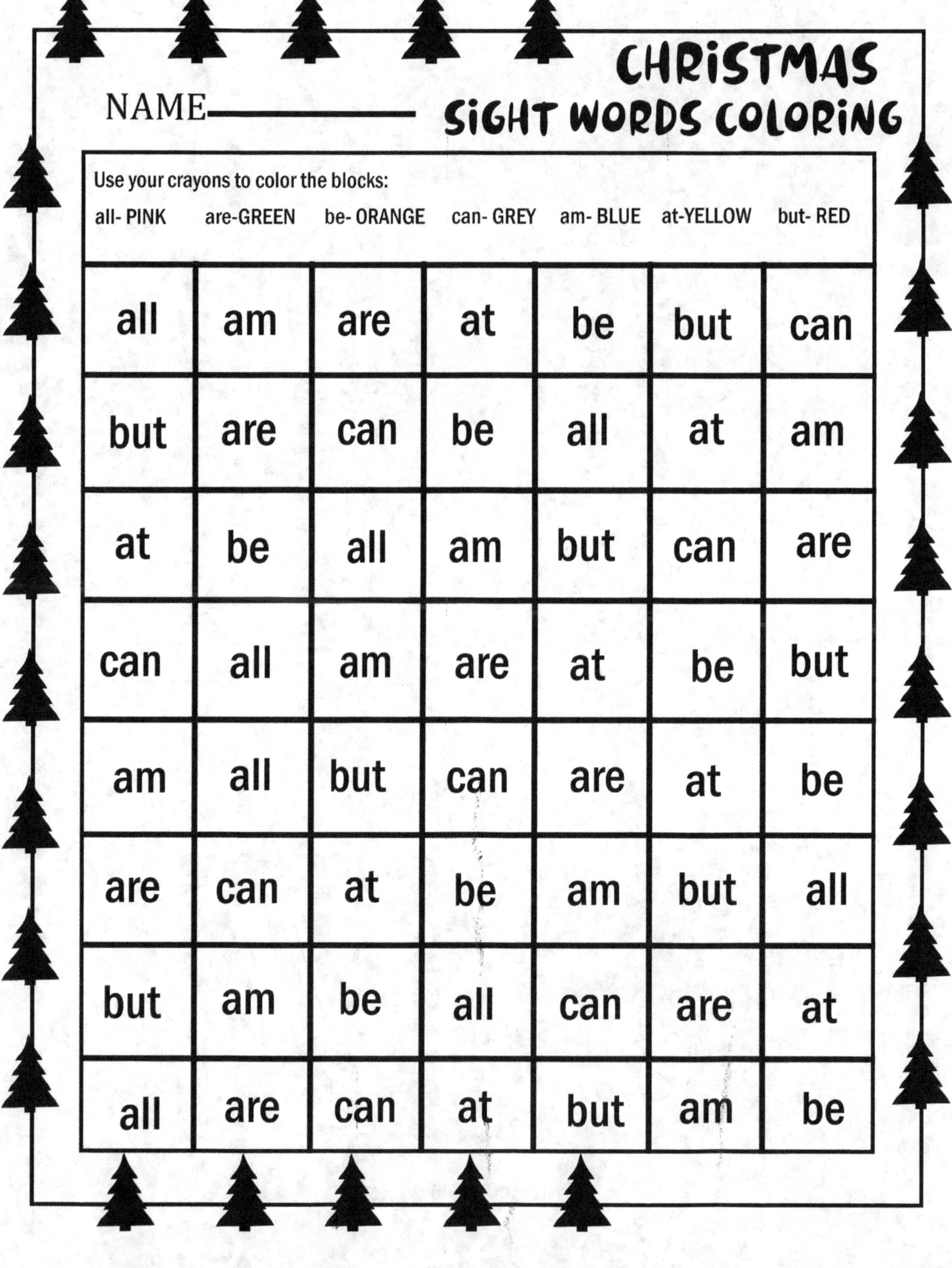

all	am	are	at	be	but	can
but	are	can	be	all	at	am
at	be	all	am	but	can	are
can	all	am	are	at	be	but
am	all	but	can	are	at	be
are	can	at	be	am	but	all
but	am	be	all	can	are	at
all	are	can	at	but	am	be

CHRISTMAS SIGHT WORDS COLORING

are- RED   at-BLUE   but- YELLOW   and- ORANGE

CHRISTMAS
SIGHT WORDS COLORING

NAME————————

Use your crayons to color the blocks:

and- PINK   go-GREEN   he- ORANGE   is- GREY   for- BLUE   had-YELLOW   in- RED

and	go	he	is	for	had	in
go	and	for	had	in	is	he
is	go	and	in	had	he	for
and	for	is	he	in	had	go
in	had	go	and	he	is	for
had	in	he	is	for	and	go
go	and	is	for	had	in	he
and	had	in	go	he	for	is

Christmas Sight Words Coloring

CHRISTMAS SIGHT WORDS COLORING

NAME————————

Use your crayons to color the blocks:

it- PINK	like-GREEN	look- ORANGE	me- GREY	my- BLUE	on-YELLOW	see- RED
it	like	look	me	my	on	see
me	on	it	look	see	like	my
look	see	like	my	me	it	on
my	on	me	it	look	see	like
it	look	my	see	like	on	me
me	see	like	on	it	my	look
my	it	see	look	on	like	me
like	on	look	me	my	see	it

CHRISTMAS SIGHT WORDS
COLORING

had- RED   **in-BLUE**   **it- YELLOW**   **like- ORANGE**

CHRISTMAS SIGHT WORDS COLORING

look- RED   me-BLUE   my- YELLOW   on- ORANGE

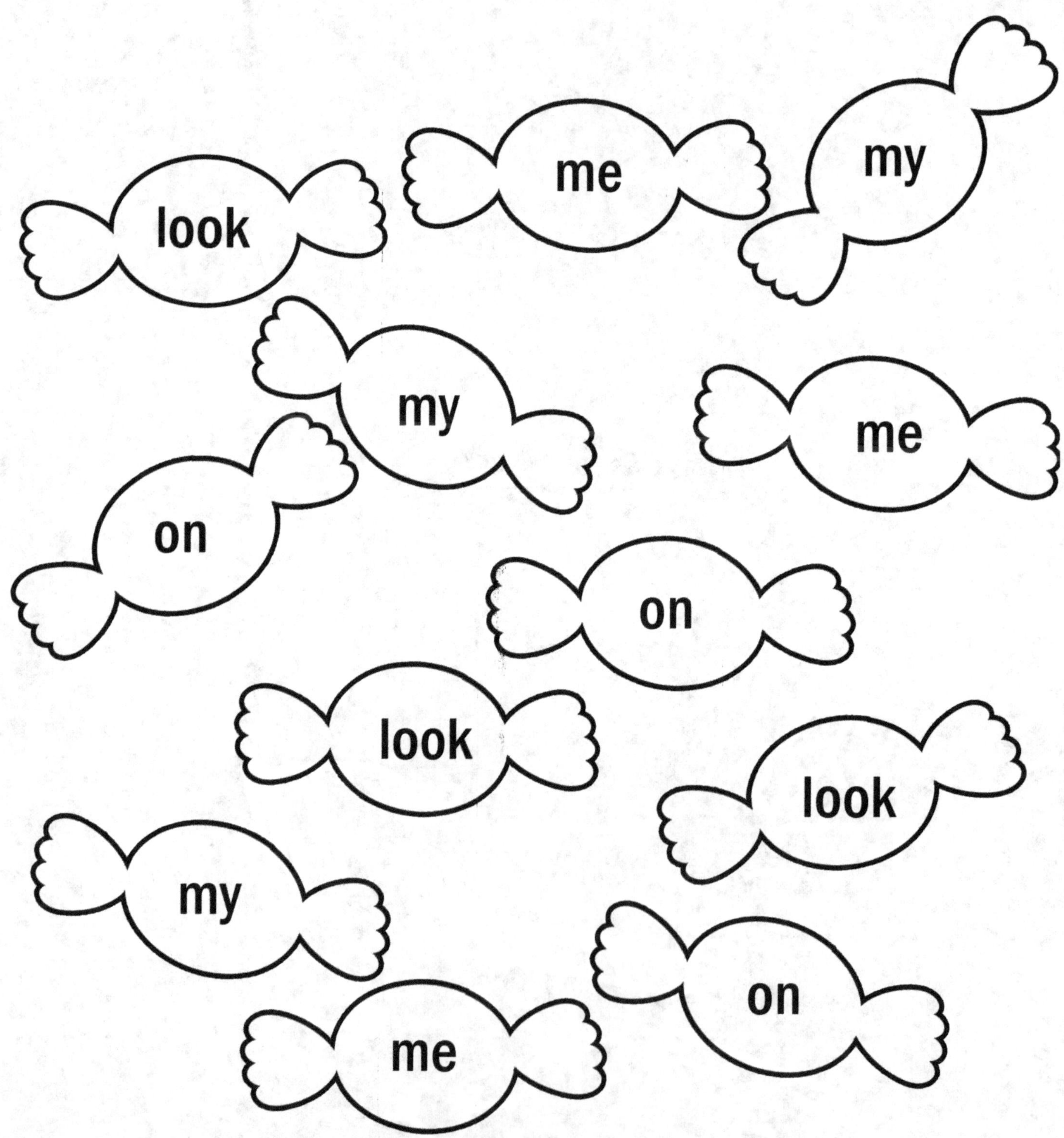

DEAR SANTA

CHRISTMAS SIGHT WORDS
COLORING

see- RED   the-BLUE   to- YELLOW   up- ORANGE

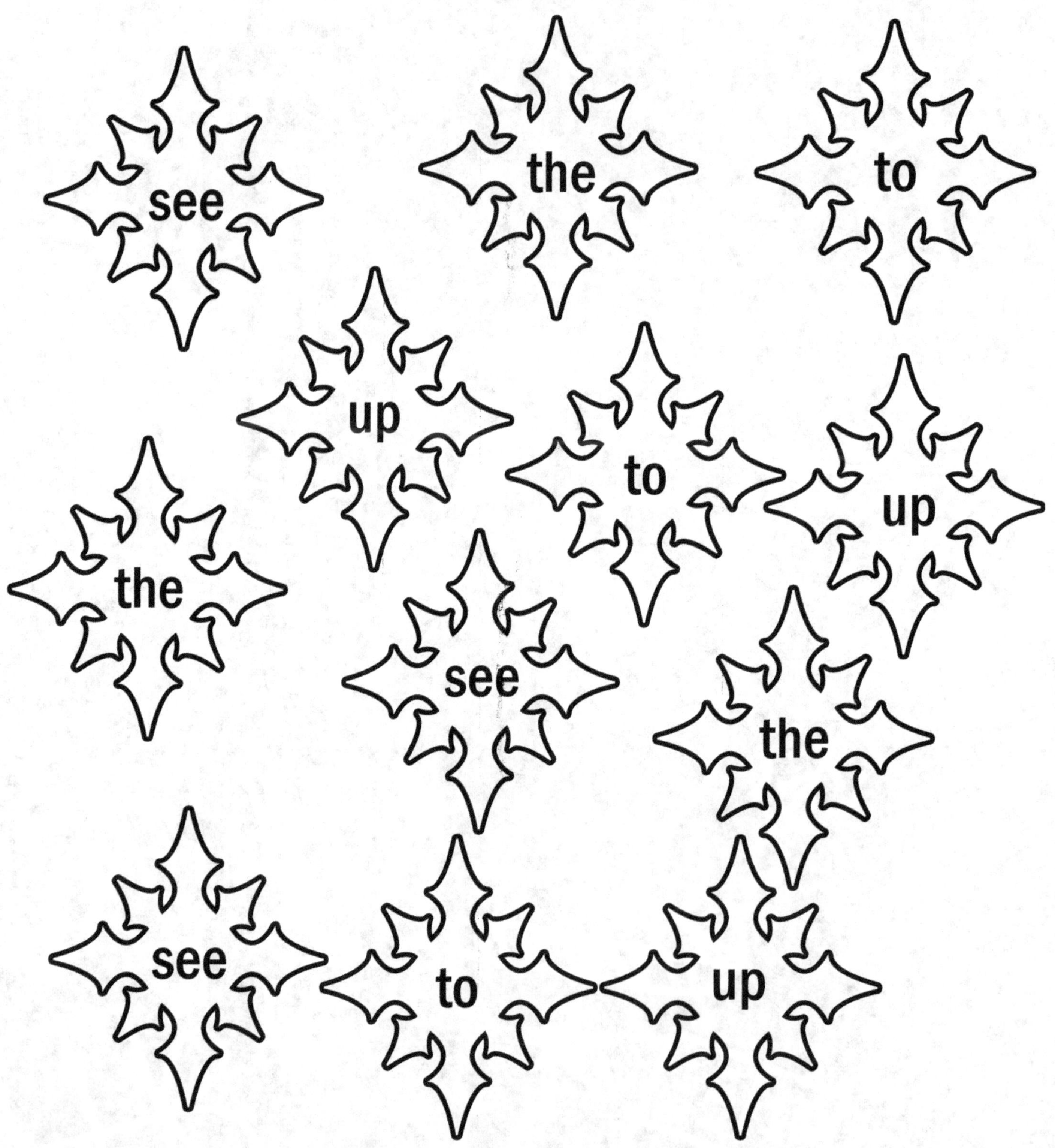

CHRISTMAS SIGHT WORDS COLORING

yes- RED   **no-BLUE**   **or- YELLOW**   **of- ORANGE**

CHRISTMAS SIGHT WORDS COLORING

did- RED   do-BLUE   eat-YELLOW   get- ORANGE

did

do

eat

eat

get

did

get

do

eat

do

did

get

CHRISTMAS SIGHT WORDS
COLORING

our- RED   out-BLUE   so- YELLOW   we- ORANGE

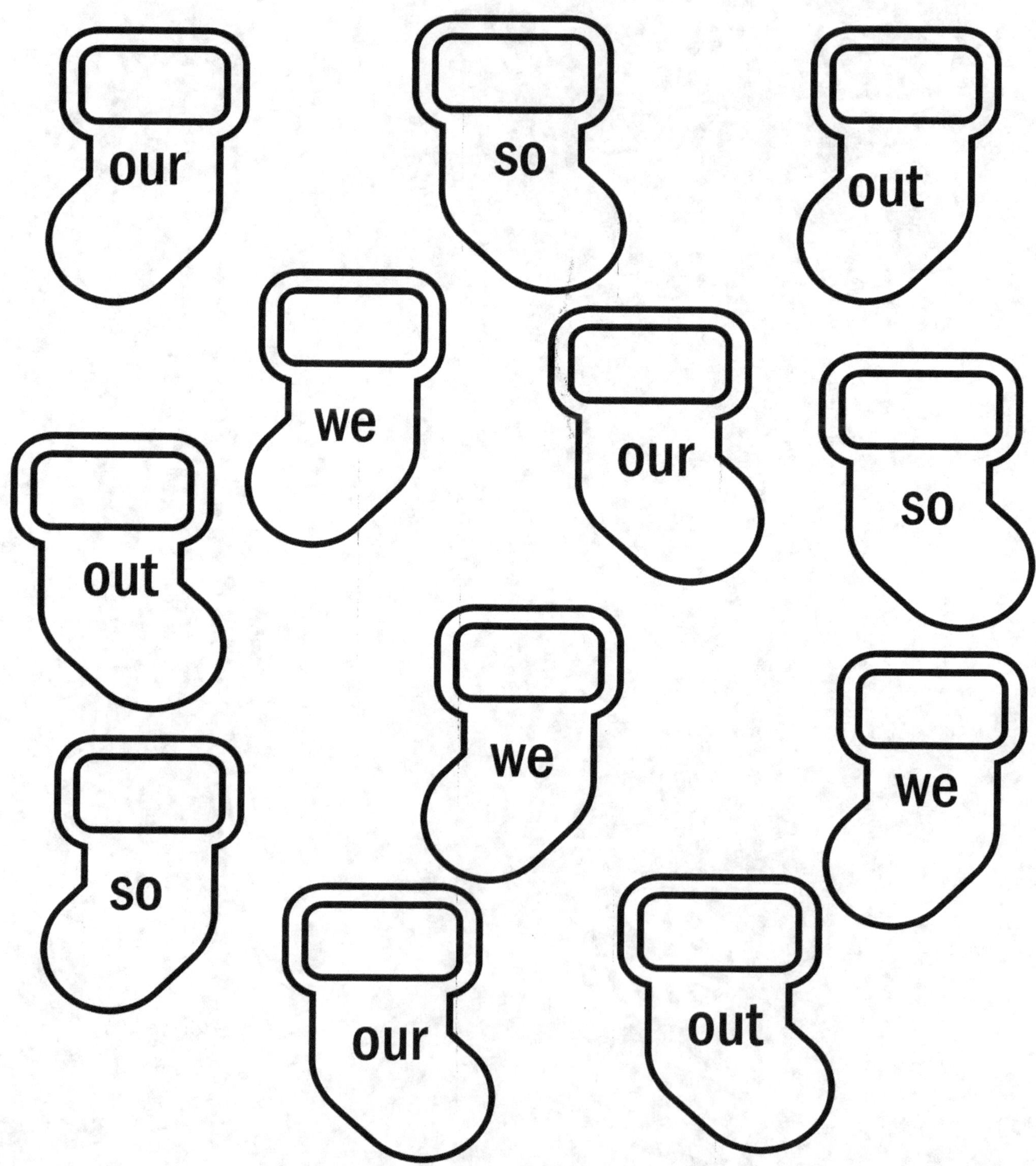

CHRISTMAS SIGHT WORDS
COLORING

us- RED   was-BLUE   big- YELLOW   one- ORANGE

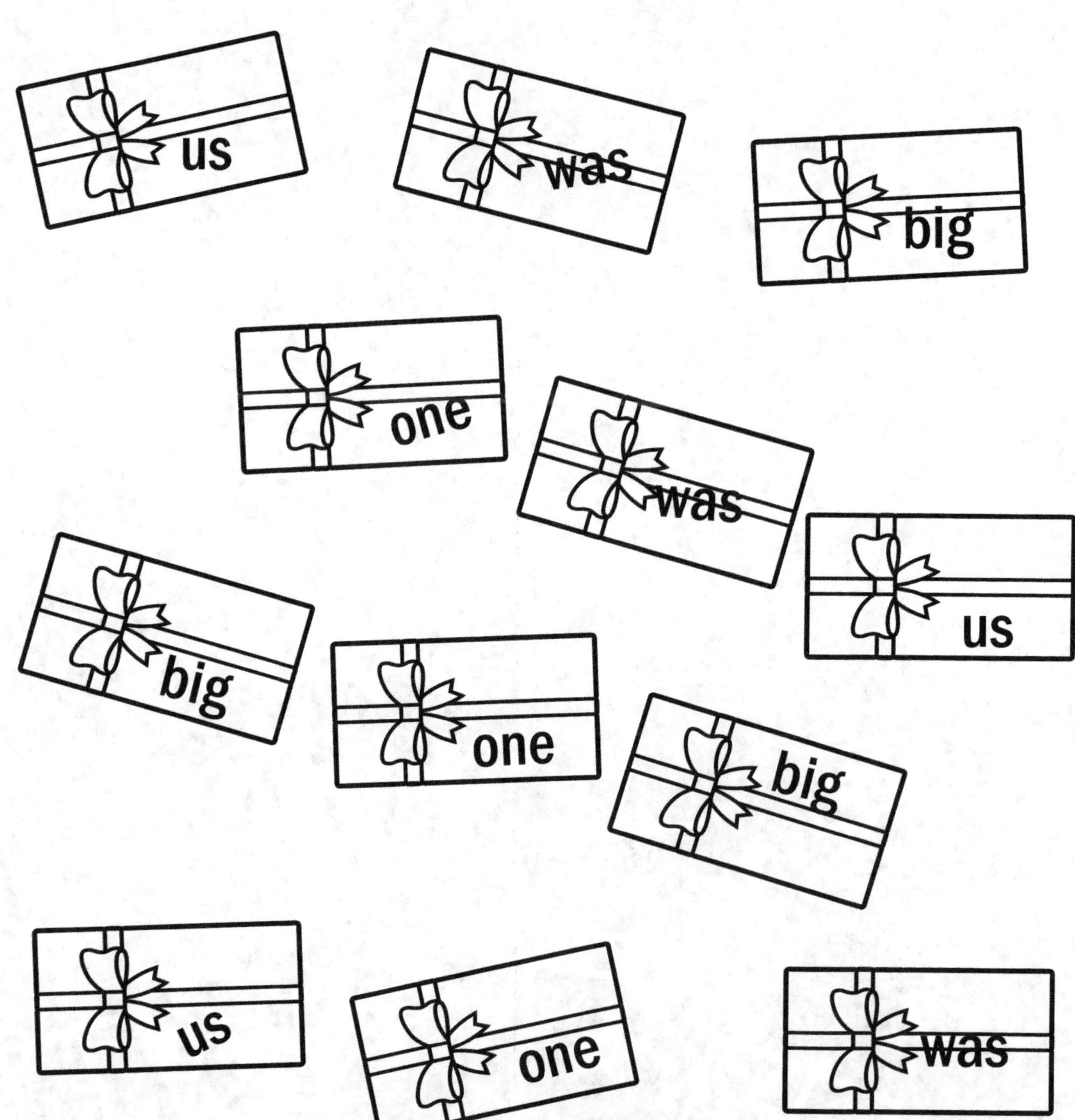

CHRISTMAS SIGHT WORDS COLORING

has- RED **as-BLUE** **ten- YELLOW** **with- ORANGE**

CHRISTMAS SIGHT WORDS COLORING

her- RED   him- BLUE   when- YELLOW   why- ORANGE

CHRISTMAS SIGHT WORDS
COLORING

who- RED   soon-BLUE   this- YELLOW   too- ORANGE

who

soon

this

soon

who

this

too

this

too

too

soon

who